A PUFFIN BOOK

PROPERTY OF

_____

_____

EDWARD ARDIZZONE was born in 1900, the eldest of five children. He went to evening classes at the Westminster School of Art and became a professional painter. Several of his pictures have been bought by the Tate Gallery. During World War II he was one of the six official war artists. He illustrated more than 200 books and was awarded the Kate Greenaway Medal for *Tim All Alone*. He was awarded the CBE in 1971 and died in 1979.

AINGELDA ARDIZZONE lives in Kent. When she told this story to her children, she was persuaded by her father-in-law, Edward Ardizzone, to write it down. What was more he offered to illustrate it! Now it is read to her grandchildren.

Aingelda studied at the Slade School of Fine Art and is a painter. A later story, *The Night Ride*, is also illustrated by Edward Ardizzone.

EDWARD & AINGELDA ARDIZZONE

The *Little Girl*
and the
Tiny Doll

PUFFIN

PUFFIN BOOKS

UK | USA | Canada | Ireland | Australia
India | New Zealand | South Africa

Puffin Books is part of the Penguin Random House group of companies
whose addresses can be found at global.penguinrandomhouse.com.

puffinbooks.com

Penguin
Random House
UK

First published in Great Britain by Longman Young Books 1966
Published in Puffin Books 1979
Published in this edition 2015
001

Text copyright © Aingelda Ardizzone, 1966
Illustrations copyright © Edward Ardizzone, 1966
All rights reserved

Set in 13.5/20.5 Sabon LT Std
Typeset by Jouve (UK), Milton Keynes
Printed in Great Britain by Clays Ltd, St Ives plc

British Library Cataloguing in Publication Data
A CIP catalogue record for this book is available from the British Library

ISBN: 978-0-141-35944-1

www.greenpenguin.co.uk

MIX
Paper from
responsible sources
FSC
www.fsc.org FSC® C018179

Penguin Books is committed to a sustainable
future for our business, our readers and our planet.
This book is made from Forest Stewardship
Council™ certified paper.

To Miss Irene Theobald

There was once a tiny doll who
belonged to a girl who did not care
for dolls so her life was very dull.

For a long time she lay forgotten
in a mackintosh pocket until one
rainy day when the girl was
out shopping.

The girl was following her
mother round a grocer's shop
when she put her hand in

her pocket and felt something
hard. She took it out and saw it
was the doll.

'Ugly old thing,' she said and
quickly put it back again, as she
thought, into her pocket.

But, in fact, it fell unnoticed into the deep freeze container among the frozen peas.

The tiny doll lay quite still for a long time,

wondering what was to become of her.

She felt so sad, partly because
she did not like being called ugly
and partly because she was lost.

5

It was very cold in the deep freeze
and the tiny doll began to feel rather
stiff, so she decided to walk about
and have a good look at the place.

The floor was crisp and white
just like frost on a winter's morning.

6

There were many packets of peas
piled one on top of the other.
They seemed to her like great
big buildings. The cracks between
the piles were rather like
narrow streets.

She walked one way and then the
other, passing, not only packets of
peas, but packets of sliced beans,
spinach, broccoli and mixed
vegetables. Then she turned a corner

8

and found herself among beef
rissoles and fish fingers. However, she
did not stop but went on exploring
until she came to boxes of strawberries;
and then ice cream.

The strawberries reminded her of
the time when she was lost once
before among the strawberry plants
in a garden.

Then she sat all day in the sun
smelling and eating strawberries.
Now she made herself as
comfortable as possible.

But it was not easy as the customers
kept taking boxes out to buy them and

the shop people would put new ones in
and not always very carefully, either.

At times it was quite frightening.
Once she was nearly squashed by a
box of fish fingers.

The tiny doll had no idea how
long she spent in the deep freeze.

Sometimes it seemed very quiet.
This, she supposed, was when the
shop was closed for the night.

She could not keep count of the days.

One day when she was busy
eating ice cream out of a packet,
she suddenly looked up and saw a
little girl she had never seen before.

The little girl was sorry for the tiny
doll and longed to take her home
to be with her other dolls.

The doll looked so cold and lonely,
but the girl did not dare to pick
her up because she had been told
not to touch things in the shop.

However, she felt she must do
something to help the doll and as
soon as she got home she set to
work to make her some warm clothes.

First of all, she made her a warm
bonnet out of a piece of red flannel.
This was a nice and easy thing to
start with.

After tea that day she asked mother
to help her cut out a coat from a
piece of blue velvet.

She stitched away so hard that
she had just time to finish it before
she went to bed.

It was very beautiful.

The next day her mother said they
were going shopping, so the little
girl put the coat and bonnet in an
empty matchbox and tied it into
a neat parcel with brown paper
and string.

She held the parcel tightly in her
hand as she walked along
the street, hurrying as she went.
She longed to know if the tiny doll
would still be there.

As soon as she reached the shop
she ran straight to the deep freeze
to look for her.

At first she could not see her anywhere.
Then, suddenly, she saw her, right
at the back, playing with the peas.

The tiny doll was throwing them
into the air and hitting them with
an ice-cream spoon.

It was a very dull game but it was
something to do.

The little girl threw in the parcel and
the doll at once started to untie it.

She looked very pleased when she
saw what was inside.

She tried on the coat, and it fitted.
She tried on the bonnet and it fitted
too. She was very pleased.

She jumped up and down with
excitement and waved to the little
girl to say thank you.

She felt so much better in warm
clothes and it made her feel happy to
think that somebody cared for her.

Then she had an idea. She made
the matchbox into a bed and
pretended that the brown paper was
a great big blanket.

With the string she wove a mat to
go beside the bed.

At last she settled down in the
matchbox, wrapped herself in the
brown paper blanket and went to sleep.

She had a long, long sleep because she
was very tired and, when she woke up,
she found that the little girl had been

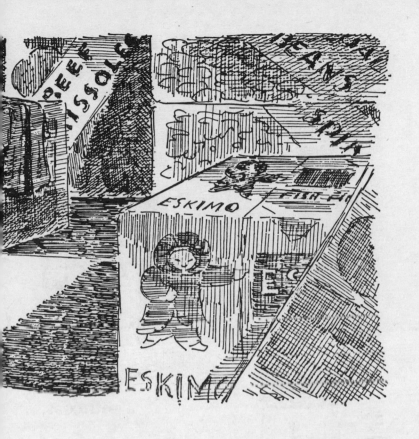

back again and had left another
parcel. This time it contained a yellow
scarf. She had always wanted a scarf.

Now the little girl came back to the
shop every day and each time she brought
something new for the tiny doll.

She made her
a sweater,

a petticoat,

knickers with tiny frills,

and gave her a little bit of looking-
glass to see herself in.

She also gave her some red tights
which belonged to one of her own
dolls to see if they would fit. They
fitted perfectly.

At last the tiny doll was beautifully
dressed and looked quite cheerful,
but still nobody except the little girl
ever noticed her.

'Couldn't we ask someone about the
doll?' the little girl asked her mother.
'I would love to take her home to
play with.'

The mother said she would ask
the lady at the cash desk when they
went to pay for their shopping.

38

'Do you know about the doll in the deep freeze?'

'No, indeed,' the lady replied. 'There are no dolls in this shop.'

39

'Oh yes there are,' said the little
girl and her mother, both at once.

So the lady from the cash desk, the
little girl and her mother all marched

off to have a look.

And there, sure enough, was the
tiny doll down among the frozen peas,
looking cold and bored.

'It's not much of a life for a doll in
there,' said the shop lady picking up
the doll and giving it to the little girl.
'You had better take her home
where she will be out of mischief.'

Having said this, she marched back
to her desk with rather a haughty
expression.

The little girl took the tiny doll
home, where she lived for many
happy years in a beautiful doll's
house. The little girl loved her and
played with her a great deal.

44

But, best of all, she liked the company
of the other dolls, because they
all loved to listen to her stories
about the time when she lived in
the deep freeze.

THE END

Extra!

Extra!

READ ALL ABOUT IT!

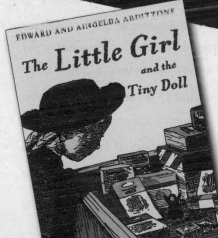

EDWARD AND AINGELDA ARDIZZONE

The **Little Girl**
and the
Tiny Doll

The Little Girl and the Tiny Doll *was written by Aingelda Ardizzone and illustrated by her father-in-law, Edward Ardizzone.*

1900 *Edward Ardizzone is born in Haiphong, Vietnam (which was then known as Tonkin)*

1905 *The Ardizzone family arrives in England*

1913–18 *Edward attends Clayesmore School in Dorset*

1927 *Aingelda is born in London*

1931 *Edward's son Philip Ardizzone is born – Edward's Little Tim picture-book stories are written for him. Aingelda grows up in Surrey countryside*

1940 *Edward is appointed Official War Artist during World War II*

1949 *Aingelda attends Slade School of Fine Art in London*

1954 *Edward is commissioned to paint a portrait of the prime minister, Sir Winston Churchill*

1954–57	*Aingelda teaches art*
1956	*Edward's book* Tim All Alone *wins the first ever Kate Greenaway Medal for the year's most distinguished work in children's book illustration. Aingelda marries Philip Ardizzone*
1966	*Aingelda writes* The Little Girl and the Tiny Doll, *which is published with Edward's illustrations*
1971	*Edward is awarded the CBE*
1973	The Night Ride, *written by Aingelda and illustrated by Edward, is published*
1978	*Philip Ardizzone dies*
1979	*Edward Ardizzone dies in Rodmersham Green, Kent*
2015	*Aingelda lives in Kent*

INTERESTING FACTS

After he left school, Edward Ardizzone worked as an office clerk. He got so bored that he doodled all over his ink-blotter!

So, he attended evening classes at the Westminster School of Art, and eventually went on to become a professional artist.

The Little Girl and the Tiny Doll is dedicated to an old family friend who came to help Aingelda with the children so that she could find time to write.

WHERE DID THE
STORY COME FROM?

Aingelda used to think of stories to tell to her children at bedtime, and The Little Girl and the Tiny Doll *is one of those stories. Her children enjoyed it so much that Aingelda's father-in-law, Edward Ardizzone, encouraged her to write it down and offered to illustrate it!*

GUESS WHO?

A   'Ugly old thing . . .'

B   It made her feel happy to think that somebody cared for her.

C   'I would love to take her home to play with.'

D   'It's not much of a life for a doll in there.'

WORDS GLORIOUS WORDS!

Lots of words have several different meanings — here are a few you'll find in this Puffin book. Use a *dictionary* or look them up online to find other definitions.

bonnet *a little hat that ties up under the chin, usually worn by babies*

grocer *someone who sells a variety of food and household items*

haughty *rather proud and stuck-up*

mischief *naughty, playful behaviour*

petticoat *an underskirt often made with a lacy edge*

velvet *a thick, shiny material which feels soft and smooth*

QUIZ

Thinking caps on – let's see how much you can remember! Answers are at the bottom of the opposite page. (No peeking!)

1 *What does the tiny doll get dropped into?*

a) *A jam jar*

b) *A freezer*

c) *A bathtub*

d) *A pocket*

2 *What does the little girl not make for the tiny doll?*

a) *A sweater*

b) *A tutu*

c) *A blue velvet coat*

d) *A bonnet*

3 *What did the tiny doll nearly get squashed by?*

a) *A box of fish fingers*

b) *The little girl's mother*

c) *Some giant strawberries*

d) *Some tins of baked beans*

4 *What does the little girl put the tiny doll's clothes in?*

a) *A teacup*

b) *Her pocket*

c) *A matchbox*

d) *Her purse*

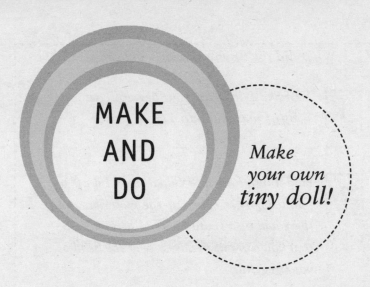

MAKE AND DO

Make your own tiny doll!

Peg dolls are very easy and fun to make.

YOU WILL NEED:

* *a wooden dolly peg (available in most craft stores)*
* *some scraps of material*
* *a ribbon*
* *some strands of wool*
* *scissors*
* *glue*
* *a thin-tipped marker pen*

1 To make a dress for your peg doll, cut a scrap of material into a small circle.

2 Fold it into four, and snip a small bit off the pointed corner. Open up the material, and there will be a small hole in the middle so that you can put the dress over the head of your peg doll.

3 Use the ribbon to make a belt.

4 Draw on a smiley face using the marker pen. (Tip: practise drawing the face on a piece of paper first.)

5 Finally, glue the strands of wool on to the doll's head to make her hair.

It's so simple – you could make a whole family!

IN
THIS YEAR

1966
Fact Pack

What else was happening in the world when this Puffin book was published?

Roald Dahl's The Magic Finger *is published.*

Miniskirts *are in fashion.*

England wins *the football* **world cup**, *beating Germany 4–2.*

The introduction of GE's relatively compact and lightweight Porta-Color **television sets** *means colour television becomes more* **popular**.

PUFFIN
WRITING
TIP

From A to Z, write a *word* that goes with every letter in the alphabet. Then, pick your favourite to *write* about!

If you have enjoyed *The Little Girl and the Tiny Doll* you may like to read *Stig of the Dump* by Clive King in which Barney makes a very remarkable friend.

1. The Ground Gives Way

IF YOU went too near the edge of the chalk pit the ground would give way. Barney had been told this often enough. Everybody had told him. His grandmother, every time he came to stay with her. His sister, every time she wasn't telling him something else. Barney had a feeling, somewhere in his middle, that it was probably true about the ground giving way. But still, there was a difference between being told and seeing it happen. And today was one of those grey days when there was nothing to do, nothing to play, and nowhere to go. Except to the chalk pit. The dump.

Barney got through the rickety fence and went to the edge of the pit. This had been the side of a hill once, he told himself. Men had come to dig away chalk and left this huge hole in the earth. He thought of all the sticks of chalk they must have made, and all the blackboards in all the schools they must have written on. They must have dug and dug for hundreds of years. And then they got tired of digging, or somebody had told them to stop before they dug away all the hill. And now they did not know what to do with this empty hole and they were trying to fill it up again. Anything people didn't want they threw into the bottom of the pit.

He crawled through the rough grass and peered over. The sides of the pit were white chalk, with lines of flints poking out like bones in places. At the top was crumbly brown earth and the roots of the trees that grew on the edge. The roots looped over the edge, twined in the air and grew back into the earth. Some of the trees hung over the edge, holding on desperately by a few roots. The earth and chalk had fallen away beneath them, and one day they too would fall to the bottom of the pit. Strings of ivy and the creeper called Old Man's Beard hung in the air.

Far below was the bottom of the pit. The dump. Barney could see strange bits of wreckage among the moss and elder bushes and nettles. Was that the steering wheel of a ship? The tail of an aeroplane? At least there was a real bicycle. Barney felt sure he could make it go if only he could get at it. They didn't let him have a bicycle.

Barney wished he was at the bottom of the pit.

And the ground gave way.

Barney felt his head going down and his feet going up. There was a rattle of falling earth beneath him. Then he was falling, still clutching the clump of grass that was falling with him.

This is what it's like when the ground gives way, thought Barney. Then he seemed to turn a complete somersault in the air, bumped into a ledge of chalk halfway down, crashed through some creepers and ivy and branches, and landed on a bank of moss.

His thoughts did those funny things they do when you bump your head and you suddenly find yourself thinking about what you had for dinner last Tuesday, all mixed up with seven times six. Barney lay with his eyes shut, waiting for his thoughts to stop being mixed up. Then he opened them.

He was lying in a kind of shelter. Looking up he could see a roof, or part of a roof, made of elder branches, a very rotten old carpet, and rusty old sheets of iron. There was a big hole, through which he must have fallen. He could see the white walls of the cliff, the trees and creepers at the top, and the sky with clouds passing over it.

Barney decided he wasn't dead. He didn't even seem to be very much hurt. He turned his head and looked around him. It was dark in this den after looking at the white chalk, and he couldn't see what sort of a place it was. It seemed to be partly a cave dug into the chalk, partly a shelter built out over the mouth of the cave. There was a cool, damp smell. Woodlice and earwigs dropped from the roof where he had broken through it.

But what had happened to his legs? He couldn't sit up when he tried to. His legs wouldn't move. Perhaps I've broken them, Barney thought. What shall I do then? He looked at his legs to see if they were all right, and found they were all tangled up with creeper from the face of the cliff. Who tied me up? thought Barney. He kicked his legs to try to get them free, but it was no use, there were yards of creeper trailing down from the cliff. I suppose I got tangled up when I fell, he thought. Expect I would have broken my neck if I hadn't.

He lay quiet and looked around the cave again. Now that his eyes were used to it he could see further into the dark part of the cave.

There was somebody there!

Or Something!

Something, or Somebody, had a lot of shaggy black hair and two bright black eyes that were looking very hard at Barney.

'Hallo!' said Barney.

Something said nothing.

'I fell down the cliff,' said Barney.

Somebody grunted.

'My name's Barney.'

Somebody-Something made a noise that sounded like 'Stig'.

'D'you think you could help me undo my feet, Mr Stig?' asked Barney politely. 'I've got a pocket-knife,' he added, remembering that he had in his pocket a knife he'd found among the wood-shavings on the floor of Grandfather's workshop. It was quite a good knife except that one blade had come off and the other one was broken in half and rather blunt.

Good thing I put it in my pocket, he thought. He wriggled so he could reach the knife, and managed to open the rusty half-blade. He tried to reach the creepers round his legs, but found it was difficult to cut creepers with a blunt knife when your feet are tied above your head.

The Thing sitting in the corner seemed to be interested. It got up and moved towards Barney into the light. Barney was glad to see it was Somebody after all. Funny way to dress though, he thought, rabbit-skins round the middle and no shoes or socks.

'Oh puff!' said Barney, 'I can't reach my feet. You do it, Stig!'

He handed the knife to Stig.

Stig turned it over and felt it with his strong hairy hands, and tested the edge with a thumb. Then instead of trying to cut the creepers he squatted down on the ground and picked up a broken stone.

He's going to sharpen the knife, thought Barney.

But no, it seemed more as if he was sharpening the stone. Using the hard knife to chip with, Stig was carefully flaking tiny splinters off the edge of the flint, until he had a thin sharp blade. Then he sprang up, and with two or three slashes cut through the creeper that tied Barney's feet.

Barney sat up. 'Golly!' he said. 'You *are* clever! I bet my Grandad couldn't do that, and he's *very* good at making things.'

Stig grinned. Then he went to the back of the cave and hid the broken knife under a pile of rubbish.

'My knife!' protested Barney. But Stig took no notice. Barney got up and went into the dark part of the cave.

He'd never seen anything like the collection of bits and pieces, odds and ends, bric-à-brac and old brock, that this Stig creature had lying about his den. There were stones and bones, fossils and bottles, skins and tins, stacks of sticks and hanks of string. There were motor-car tyres and hats from old scarecrows, nuts and bolts and bobbles from brass bedsteads. There was a coal scuttle full of dead electric light bulbs and a basin with rusty screws and nails in it. There was a pile of bracken and newspapers that looked as if it were used for a bed. The place looked as if it had never been given a tidy-up.

'I wish I lived here,' said Barney.